A journey . . . long ago an egg travelled . . .

TOM and the DINOSAUR EGG

written and
illustrated
by
Ian Beck

PICTURE CORGI

Tom lived with his grandfather in a lighthouse
which was surrounded by sharp rocks and wild seas.

For Pandora Dewan

TOM AND THE DINOSAUR EGG
A PICTURE CORGI BOOK 978 0 552 55414 5

First published in Great Britain by Picture Corgi,
an imprint of Random House Children's Books
A Random House Group Company

This edition published 2008

3 5 7 9 10 8 6.4 2

Text and illustrations copyright © Ian Beck, 2008

The right of Ian Beck to be identified as the author and
illustrator of this work has been asserted in accordance
with the Copyright, Designs and Patents Act 1988.

Picture Corgi Books are published by
Random House Children's Books,
61–63 Uxbridge Road, London W5 5SA

www.kidsatrandomhouse.co.uk
www.rbooks.co.uk

Addresses for companies within The Random House Group
Limited can be found at: www.randomhouse.co.uk/offices.htm

THE RANDOM HOUSE GROUP Limited Reg. No. 954009

A CIP catalogue record for this book is available from the
British Library.

Printed in China

Tom untangled it and carried it carefully back to the lighthouse.

Then he showed it to his grandfather.

Well, it might be a seabird's egg, might be a lizard's. Let's keep it nice and warm and see what happens.

Tom checked on the egg every morning . . .

and last thing at night.

Tom took his dinosaur for walks on the beach every day, and as winter turned to summer, his friend grew . . .

and grew . .

and grew . . .

and grew!

And the bigger he grew, the longer Tom's dinosaur spent gazing at the far horizon.

He belongs some-where like this.

I'm going to take you home.

Tom, the dinosaur and Grandfather worked hard to build a big enough raft.

It had a small cabin for Tom and a big sail to catch the wind.

Tom and the dinosaur set
sail the next day . . .

They caught a strong wind . . .

and they were soon surrounded by miles and miles and miles of open sea.

They sailed for weeks on many seas . . .

wild seas . . .

and stormy seas.

They sailed through the day and night.

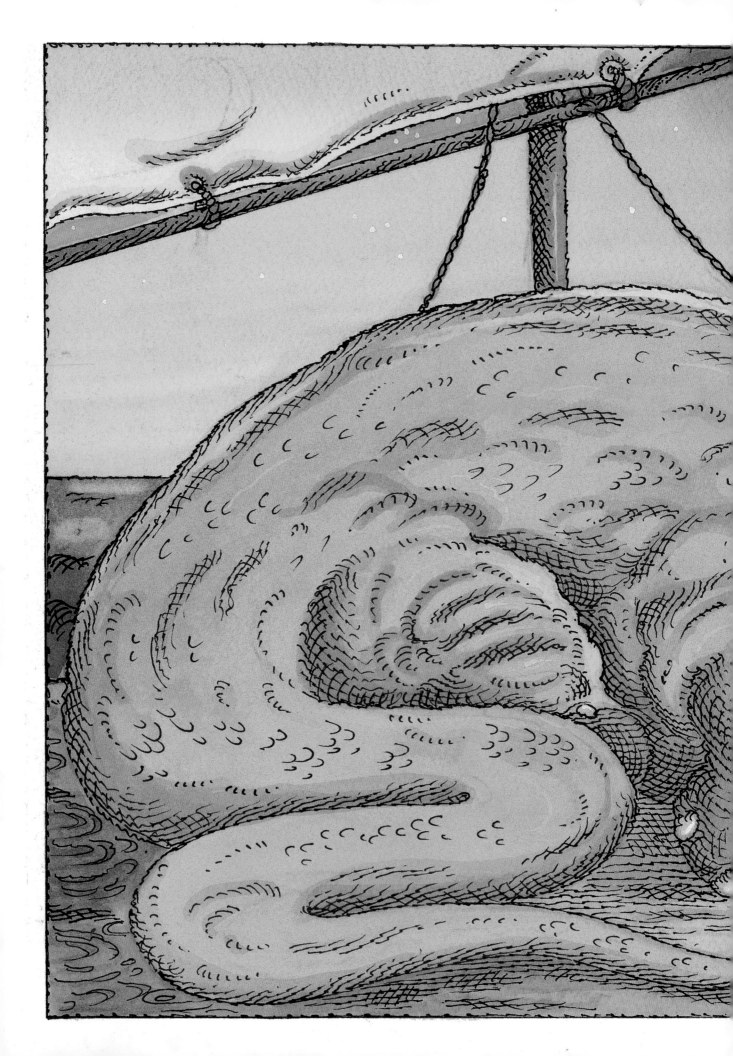

After weeks and weeks at sea the weather became warmer and the sea calmer. Tom was sure they were nearly there.

They changed direction and soon they saw another island.

It was green with trees and a jungle.

They sailed nearer to the green island . . .

The dinosaur listened to the roaring . . .

and answered with
a roar of his own.

Then he waited . . .

The dinosaur was home at last!

ROAR!

Tom hugged
his friend.

Then he waved goodbye
and set sail for home.

He sailed back alone
through the sun . . .

and the wind . . .

and the storms, until he finally
saw the lighthouse light.

and Tom told him of
his adventures.

Grandfather welcomed him back
from his long voyage . . .

It was
amazing!